MW01147758

THANKSGIVING DELI MURDER

THE DARLING DELI SERIES, BOOK 28

PATTI BENNING

SUMMER PRESCOTT BOOKS PUBLISHING

CHAPTER ONE

Moira Darling stood on her front porch with her hands on her hips, considering the carpet of dead and dry leaves that littered her front yard. *I could get the rake out of the garage*, she thought. If her yard was smaller, she might have done it despite the chilly breeze, but the grass extended around the house, and it would have taken hours to complete it on her own, especially if the wind began to gust.

Lawnmower it is, she thought, turning to go back inside as the wind raised goosebumps on her arms. She would have to call the young man who mowed their yard and ask him to come back out one last time that season to turn the leaves into mulch before it started to snow. She loved living in the little stone house in the woods, but maintaining the yard wasn't as easy as it had been when she lived in town. There, she and her daughter, Candice, had been able to simply take turns with the push mower once a week during the summer to keep the grass looking nice, and it had been simple to shovel their short driveway in the winter. Now, with a much bigger yard and longer driveway, she found herself relying on others more than she would like to at times.

"We'll buy a riding lawn mower next year," she said to herself as she slipped off her shoes just inside the door. Talking to herself was a habit that she had gotten into, and it seemed difficult to break. With David working two jobs, he was rarely home during the day. That left her with her two dogs as conversation partners, and they rarely answered back.

Her life seemed to alternate between being unbelievably busy, and dull. With her daughter living in another town, and her two best friends busy with their own families and relationships, her main focus was work, and the deli had been running smoothly lately. So smoothly that it hardly seemed to need her attention.

Helping David run his private investigating business helped give her something to do on the slower days, but they hadn't had a new client in over a week. It was at times like these that she wanted to do something more with her life. David had his career as a private investigator and his growing microbrewery, and it made her itch to begin to work on growing the deli.

However, when things picked up and she was busy with hiring, helping her friends, or working mornings at her husband's office, she was glad that she had these slow times to fall back on.

Moira went into the kitchen and wrote a note to remind herself about the lawn. She stuck it on the fridge, then started scrubbing the coffee pot, pouring the dregs of that morning's coffee out in the sink. Her two dogs, Maverick the German Shepherd, and Keeva the Irish wolfhound, lay on the kitchen floor, watching her through half closed eyes.

It was a peaceful morning, quiet and warm in the house despite the wind blowing outside. Moira found herself fighting back a yawn as she finished the dishes.

"Okay, guys, I need to start getting ready to go," she said. "I'm going to fall asleep if I don't do something."

She dried her hands, then left the kitchen, the dogs following behind her as she went upstairs. She took a few seconds to choose an outfit out of her closet, finally settling on a soft maroon sweater and a pair of comfortable dark jeans. One of the benefits of owning her own business meant that she never had to dress up if she didn't want to. Her customers didn't care if she served them soup and sandwiches in jeans, and she saw no reason to be any less comfortable than she had to be.

. . .

She said goodbye to the dogs, giving them each a treat from the bowl on the kitchen counter, then headed out to the car. Her shift at the deli didn't start for another couple of hours, and she wanted to make a few of stops first.

David's microbrewery was located on a farm a few miles out of town. The property was owned by her daughter, Candice, but most of it had been leased out to neighboring farmers. The house itself had been rented to a woman named Thelma, who was related to one of Moira's employees.

Not long ago, they had discovered that Allison, the young woman who had worked for Moira for the past two years, was Candice's half-sister. They were all still reeling from the revelation, and Moira was concerned about her young employee, which was the reason for today's visit with her aunt.

She pulled up the long gravel driveway, parking in front of the farmhouse across the way from the

PATTI BENNING

brewery's parking lot. David's car was there; she would have to stop and say hi to him before she left.

She walked up to the farmhouse's front door and knocked. A moment later, it opened, and she found herself face to face with a middle-aged woman wearing a full-length apron and covered in flour.

"Hey, Thelma," she said. "Did I catch you at a bad time?"

"Oh, no. Actually, I completely forgot that you were coming over, but that's my fault. Come on in, I was just in the middle of doing some baking."

Moira followed the other woman into the house, shutting the door behind her. It was toasty inside, with a fire crackling in the old fireplace in the living room. Thelma had bought her own furniture for the house, and already had paint samples taped to the walls.

. . .

6

"It looks like you got moved in all right," she said as they walked through the house toward the kitchen.

"It's pretty much all I've been doing," Thelma admitted. "Making the pies today is my version of taking a break, believe it or not. I'm so thrilled that your daughter is fine with me painting the walls. It really helps to make a house feel like home."

"I think she's just glad that all of that old wallpaper will be gone," Moira said with a smile. "I like the colors you're looking at. This place is going to feel like new with a fresh coat of paint."

"I can't thank you enough for helping me find this place," Thelma said. "It's perfect, at least until I decide to buy a house."

"I'm glad it worked out. I think Candice was thrilled to rent to you. You're family — well, sort of."

. . .

The other woman's face fell slightly. "How is Allison doing? I keep trying to schedule lunch with her, but she always says she is busy."

"I don't know," Moira admitted with a sigh. "She comes to work, but she's not herself. She's quiet, she hardly talks to customers, and she barely says a word to me. Usually, she's the cheeriest and most talkative of us all."

"I just wish that the circumstances were different," Thelma said. "If only she hadn't been the one to find Mike... I can't even imagine how it must have affected her to find out that she discovered her own father's body."

"It hasn't been easy for her. She seemed to be doing better while Candice was here, but she just couldn't put off going home any longer."

"I'll try again to see her. I think she wants to avoid talking about it, but she can't keep whatever she's going through bottled up forever. I hope she will at least talk to her mother."

"When will she be back?"

"The cruise ends a few days after Thanksgiving. I know my sister feels terrible, but there's no way she can get back early."

Moira nodded, wondering what she would do in that situation. It would be terrible to know that her daughter was going through an emotional crisis and that she had no way to reach her.

"I'll try to talk to her, too," Moira said. "I know I'm not really family, but she's related to my daughter. That has to mean something."

"I'm sure one of us will be able to reach her, eventually." Thelma sighed and began to roll out a pie crust. Moira looked around the kitchen.

. . .

"How many pies are you making?"

"Too many," Thelma said. "I went a little bit over-board, but I figure I can give them to people. I've got a couple of apple pies with your name on them."

"I bet they're delicious," Moira said. "I know David will appreciate them, too. Thank you."

"Of course. With everything you've done to help me out, you deserve more than just a few pies, but it will have to do for now. Let me know if Allison talks to you, okay? I really am worried about her.

"I will." She was worried about the young woman too. Only time would tell how she handled the news about her father. Moira knew that processing and healing from the shock would take some time; she just hoped Allison didn't do anything she might regret in the meantime.

CHAPTER TWO

After saying a quick hello to David at the microbrewery, Moira drove straight to the deli. It was almost noon, and their lunch hours had started. Lunch was always a busier time of day than breakfast, and she didn't want to leave her employees shorthanded, especially with Allison still struggling with her own issues.

She took her usual spot right in front of the building — another perk of being the owner — and went inside. Nearly half of the tables were taken, and there was a healthy hum of conversation in the dining area. Cold weather seemed to make people crave warm comfort foods, and almost everyone had a steaming bowl of soup in front of them.

"Hey, Ms. D.," one of her employees said, looking up from the register.

"Hi, Darrin," she said. "How are things going?"

"It was a slow morning, but it's started to pick up. I'm just about to clock out, unless there's something you want me to do first."

"Nope, you're free to go. Is Allison here?"

"She's in the back. She didn't want to work the register today. We got the black bean soup going, and I did most of the breakfast dishes, other than the last pan of quiches."

"I'll see if anyone wants them for half price, and if

not, I'll put them in the fridge for you guys to snack on. Enjoy your afternoon off."

"I will," he replied, giving her a smile before typing his code into the register to officially get off the clock.

Moira took her place at the register and helped the next few customers. Once the line was clear, she slipped into the kitchen to greet Allison. She found the younger woman standing at the stove, slowly stirring the simmering pot of black bean soup.

"I hope it wasn't too hard to make," Moira said, setting her purse down on the table. Recently she had felt like she had to tiptoe around the other woman. She wanted to ask her directly how she was doing, but was worried about how Allison would react.

"It was fine," her employee said.

· · ·

"How has your day been?"

Allison shrugged. "Is that guy gone yet?"

"Darrin?" Moira asked, blinking. Allison had known Darrin for years. It didn't make sense that she would refer to him as "that guy," but she couldn't think of who else her employee might be referring to.

"No," Allison said, turning to face Moira for the first time and giving her an odd look. "The guy who has been snooping around the deli all morning."

Moira raised her eyebrows. "Darrin didn't mention anything about someone snooping around. Why didn't one of you call me?"

"He thought I was just being paranoid," Allison said. "Well, he said it more nicely than that. Everyone has been acting so weird around me lately."

. . .

Moira felt a pinch of guilt. It was true. Everyone who knew what Allison was going through had been treating her as if she was made of glass. It probably hadn't made things any easier for the young woman.

"I'm sorry —" she began.

"It's okay, Allison said quickly, shaking her head. I just want to know if that guy is still out there."

"Let's go see," Moira said. "Just point him out to me if he's there."

Allison put the wooden spoon that she had been using to stir the soup down and followed Moira out of the kitchen and into the dining area.

"That's him," the young woman whispered, nudging her boss and inclining her head toward a man sitting at a small bistro table in the corner. He had a drink in front of him, but no food, and was scribbling quickly in a notebook.

Moira nodded and returned to the kitchen, gesturing for Allison to follow her. "How long has he been here?" she asked once the door was shut behind them, keeping her voice low even though she knew no one else would be able to hear her.

"Since this morning," Allison said. "He was already here when I arrived for my shift. Darrin said he got here around nine. He's been ordering drinks and walking around. I saw him taking pictures, and he tried to get into the kitchen once. He said he thought it was the door to the bathroom."

Frowning, Moira said, "I'll go talk to him. I'm sure he has a perfectly good explanation, but if he doesn't, I'll ask him to leave."

"Do you think he's casing the place?" her employee

asked, looking frightened. "What if he's planning to rob us?"

"I'm sure he's not," Moira said, trying to calm the younger woman down. "I'll be right back, okay? You keep working on the soup."

Despite her own words, she couldn't help but worry that her employee might be right. It certainly sounded like the mysterious man was trying to case their restaurant. Luckily for them, he wasn't very good at doing it without attracting attention.

She went back out into the main area and walked directly over to the table where the man was sitting. He was wearing all black, including a black wool cap on his head. No wonder he had caught Allison's attention. Between his outfit and his behavior, Moira thought she would have been suspicious herself.

"Hello," she said when she reached his table. "Is

there anything else I can get you? We have mini quiches available for half price."

"No thanks," he said, barely looking up at her.

"You've been here for quite a while. Is there something we can help you with? If you need to make a call to find a ride somewhere, I'd be happy to let you use my phone."

Now he did look up at her, an expression of annoyance on his face. "I'm fine," he said. "I didn't know you had a time limit on how long people could stay. I keep making purchases, so I didn't think it would be a problem."

"It's just that you're making my employees nervous," she said. "I'm sure you can understand how they would be uncomfortable with someone taking photos of them. We've had some problems with crime over the past few years, which is why we have so many security cameras installed, as you can see."

. . .

She saw his eyes dart up to the ceiling and track into the corners, registering the camera above the register and the motion detector in the hallway that led to the bathroom. Clearing his throat, he rose from the table and tucked his notebook under his arm.

"It's time for me to get going anyway," he said. "Have a nice day."

She watched as he left the restaurant, the back of her neck prickling. Something was certainly off about him, but hopefully now that she had pointed out the security cameras and had spoken with him directly, he would be smart enough not to try anything. She might not have his name, but she knew his face and would make a mental note to save the security footage from that morning. If he did come back later in an attempt to do something illegal, she would make life very difficult for him indeed.

CHAPTER THREE

She mentioned the strange man to her other employees, and thankfully none of them spotted him again over the next few days. She still wasn't sure why he had been there, or what his plan had been, and something told her that they hadn't seen the last of him.

When Saturday dawned, she woke up feeling much more cheerful than she had the past couple of days. David had a rare day off, and she was looking forward to spending it with him.

.   .   .

She looked over at her husband, who was still sleeping, and decided to let him enjoy the chance to get some extra time to snooze. It would give her time to get started on the coffee and let the dogs out before the day really started.

The coffee maker had just stopped gurgling when David came downstairs, his hair sticking up in all directions.

"Good morning," Moira said cheerfully.

"Good morning," he replied, yawning. "The coffee smells good."

"I'll pour you a mug. What do you want to do for breakfast? We could make something here, or go out to eat."

"Which would you prefer?"

. . .

She shrugged. "I'm happy with anything. I was thinking we could take the dogs to the county park today. They have all of those nice trails, and it's going to be winter soon. I'd like to go before it gets too wet and cold."

"It's hunting season, isn't it? If we go out, we'll have to wear orange. Do you still have the vests we got for the dogs last year?"

"I think they're in the closet," she said. "I'll go check."

"Okay. Before we go on the walk, we should go out for food. I don't think I'm in the mood for breakfast, though. How about burgers? The diner opens at eleven."

They decided to wait until after lunch to take a walk. David was right, it had been a while since they had simply had a good burger and fries. Now that he had mentioned the food, Moira couldn't stop thinking of biting in to a juicy Lakeside Burgers patty.

. . .

Healthy eating, she knew, had never been their forte. David had the metabolism of a cheetah, but she didn't. Ever since Candice had been born, she had watched her weight fluctuate up to ten pounds as she gained weight, then dieted to lose it.

It may not have been the perfect way to live, but it worked for her. Food was such a big part of her life that it didn't make sense to take the enjoyment out of it if she didn't have to. She got inspiration everywhere for dishes for the deli, which meant that she had to remain open to trying new things. Or so she told herself. The truth was, she just liked food a little too much.

At the diner, a waitress told them to seat themselves. They took a worn-out booth near the window, and she approached a few minutes later to take their drink orders.

"What do you think you're going to get?" David asked as they opened their menus.

"I think the mushroom and Swiss burger looks good," Moira said. "I remember getting it before, and I think I liked it."

"I think I'm just going to get a classic bacon burger. And I'll try to save room for dessert. Their lava cakes are amazing."

Moira agreed, though she was already wondering if they would have any energy left for a walk after the meal.

"Are the two of you ready to order, or do you need more time?" the waitress asked on her return to the table.

"I think we're ready, Jeanie," Moira said, squinting at

her name tag. They placed their orders, then relaxed into conversation again while they waited for their food.

"This is nice," David said. "We should go out together more often. We used to go on dates a couple of times a week."

"I know," Moira said. "I miss it. I know that we've both been busy on and off for the past few months, but we should make time for each other."

"I'll try to be gone less," he promised, reaching across the table to squeeze her hand. "It's easy to get so drawn in to work that I forget what's really important."

"Trust me when I say I know," Moira said. "I hardly had time for anything when I was first building the deli. In a way, it's good that Candice was gone for college, because I was hardly home at all anyway."

· · ·

They talked a little bit more about their plans for Thanksgiving, and then their food came. They both fell silent as they took the first few bites. Moira had been starving, and biting into the perfect burger was heavenly.

"How is everything?" the waitress asked, coming back to the table to check on them. "I'm about to clock out for the day. Anne will be your new server, if you need anything."

"It's great, thank you," Moira said. "I love this place. Your burgers are the best."

"I'm glad to hear it," the other woman said. "I've worked here for thirty years, and I'm here almost every day. In fact, I live right next door." She chuckled. "If that's not dedication to a job, I don't know what is. Anyway, I'll pass your compliments along to the owner. He'll be glad to hear a good word from a fellow restaurant owner."

·   ·   ·

Moira raised her eyebrows in surprise, but the waitress walked away before she could say anything. She still wasn't used to people recognizing her from the deli, though by now she supposed she should be.

"That'll be you in thirty years," her husband said with a smile. "Still working at the deli."

"I hope not," Moira said, laughing. "At least not every day. I'll be in my seventies in thirty years. I hope I'll be able to retire by then, and only stop in at the deli when I get bored."

"Do you think you'll sell it?" he asked.

"I don't know," Moira admitted. "I guess when I opened it, I always thought Candice would take it over. Now, of course, she has her own dream to follow. Maybe Darrin will want it. And what about your microbrewery?"

.   .   .

"I haven't thought about that at all. I suppose if it keeps growing, I'll either sell it, or give my half to my sister and let her deal with it. If it stays small, we may just close it."

CHAPTER FOUR

After Moira and David returned home, they got the two dogs loaded up into the SUV and headed toward town. The park they wanted to go to was on the opposite side of Maple Creek, and encompassed a small lake as well as a huge forest with multiple biking and walking trails. She had been there before, but it had been a while. She wanted to see it again with David by her side.

It was a chilly day, and overcast, but the weather channel had promised that the chance of rain was low. It was late enough in the year that most of the trees were bare, with their leaves now forming a multicolored carpet on the forest floor.

. . .

She parked the car in the parking area at the park's entrance and walked around to the back, where she let Keeva and Maverick out. She passed Keeva's leash to David, then shut the hatch and pressed the button on her keys to lock the vehicle.

"Ready to go?" she asked.

"Yep. You lead the way."

She walked toward the trailhead, pausing to look at the map. She wasn't sure how long they would want to be out, and decided to go with the shortest loop the trails offered in case they got cold.

There had been a few vehicles in the parking lot, but they didn't see any sign of other people when they got into the woods. The forest was quiet, other than the occasional squirrel making a mad dash across the dry leaves.

. . .

"This is nice," David said. "It's good to get outside. I can't believe it's so late in the year already."

"Me either. It seems like it was just summer. In less than two months, it will be a new year."

"And hopefully a less busy one," he said. "With building the microbrewery, and everything that has happened with Candice, I feel like we've barely had time to catch our breaths."

"It's been a weird year," she agreed. "The deli is doing well, though, which I'm grateful for."

"Has that man come back?"

She shook her head. "No one has seen him. He was probably just some out of town visitor or something."

. . .

"You seemed pretty concerned when you mentioned him."

"I was, but worrying about who he might be won't do anything to help. As long as he doesn't come poking around again, I'm happy to forget about the entire issue."

"I still think that you should have told Detective Jefferson about him. You've had enough issues at the deli over the past few years that it's worth giving the police a heads up when something like this happens."

"While I do think that he was probably up to no good while he was there, I don't think that he will come back, and I don't want to bother Jefferson with something like that. As soon as I pointed out the cameras, he left. We have him on video – I saved the footage – and I would be able to identify him in a lineup."

. . .

"But you don't have his name," her husband said. "You can't find someone just by their face, not easily anyway."

"It's a bit late to go to the police," she said. "Even if I wanted to, they wouldn't be able to do anything about it now. If he comes back again and gives me any reason to worry, I promise I will talk to Detective Jefferson."

"Okay, I suppose that will have to be good enough for me." Her husband tightened his grip on the leash as Keeva tugged to sniff at something in the leaves. Both dogs were wearing bright orange vests. She and David were wearing orange hats, and brightly colored jackets. Hunting season in Michigan was always a big deal, and she knew that the woods would be full of hunters on the lookout for deer. However, the park was still open to hikers, and she wasn't going to sit at home all deer season when she could be out enjoying the last of the nice weather. Winter this far north in the mitten was bound to be rough, and she knew once the snow came, she would be hard-pressed to leave the house for more than a few minutes at a time.

"I know you're worried," she said to her husband after a moment. "And I can see why. I would be, too, if I were in your position. I guess I'm less worried about the deli suffering a potential theft than I am about Allison, who seemed very shaken up by the whole thing. Although to be fair, she has seemed very shaken up ever since she found out about Mike."

"How is she doing with all of that?"

"I think she's getting a little bit better," Moira said. "I just wish that she would talk to someone. I know it was hard enough on her just finding the body. Now, two years after the fact, she found out that it was her own father. That's not something that anyone is prepared to deal with. She's been avoiding her aunt, and only says what she needs to at work. I know she has spoken to Candice a few times, but I don't want to pry too much into their conversations. After all, they are sisters."

"Half-sisters," David said automatically. "At least Candice seems glad about her new relative. I'm sure she will be able to help Allison through all of this. I know you feel a connection to the girl now that you know she is related to your daughter, but I think it's important to let her real family handle it."

"You are probably right... this whole thing is just so confusing, for all of us. I feel terrible for her, and..."

She broke off as a gunshot rang through the woods. The sound made Maverick jump, and Keeva perked her ears up. Moira frowned. It had sounded close. She knew there were hunters out there, but she thought that they would stay in the area of the park that didn't have well groomed trails. Hunting shouldn't be allowed so close to where people were walking, and besides, hikers would scare away all of the animals.

· · ·

Then the screaming started. She didn't know if it was a man or an animal. It was a terrible sound. She looked over at David.

"Is... is that a deer?"

His face had gone pale. "I don't think so," he said. "That sounds like a human."

They exchanged a glance, then hurried forward toward the sound of the screams. The dogs slowed them down as their leashes got tangled in the under-growth. As they got nearer, she could make out the man's shouts for help. He sounded close, but she couldn't see him.

"I think he's over that hill," David said. "Here, you take Keeva's leash. I'll go ahead."

"I'll be right behind you," Moira said. She wasn't about to let her husband go alone.

. . .

She followed him, making sure to keep a firm grip on the dogs' leashes. They were both straining forward, whining anxiously. She fumbled to pull her phone out of her pocket. By the sound of it, someone was hurt badly enough to need an ambulance. She had one bar of service. Hopefully, it would be enough for an emergency call.

She saw David reach the top of the hill and freeze. Panting, she hurried up beside him. Looking down, she could see what had made him stop. The man was there, but he had fallen silent. He was slouched against a log, wearing hunter's orange on his head and a camouflage jacket. There was a rifle by his unmoving hand, and Moira could see the glow of a cell phone's screen in the leaves.

"Is he dead?"

David shook his head. "I don't know. I'm going to go down and see if I can help him. You call the police. If

39

he is still alive, he needs an ambulance as soon as possible."

CHAPTER FIVE

With shaking fingers, she dialed 911 as David hurried down the steep hill. Just as he reached the man, an operator answered her call.

"I need an ambulance," she said. "Someone's been shot." She did her best to tell them exactly where they were, but was unable to tell him whether or not the man was still alive. She hesitated, then put the phone down and tied the dogs' leashes to a small tree. Picking the phone back up, she made her way down the hill toward David.

"Is he breathing?" she asked.

. . .

"Just barely," David said. "Take off your jacket. I need something to stop the blood."

She shrugged off her jacket and handed it over to David, then related the information to the emergency line's operator. She watched, horrified and helpless, as her husband tried to stop the bleeding from the man's chest. She didn't know how long they had been sitting there, but at last she realized that there was a voice coming from her phone. The operator was still on the line, and was asking her to meet the paramedics on the trail so she could guide them to where the injured man was. Telling David that she would be right back with help, she walked back up the hill, grabbed the dogs, and found her way back to the trail. Minutes later, she met with the paramedics, and hurried to return to the site of the gunshot victim.

She could tell as soon as she crested the hill that the news wasn't good. David was sitting back with blood on his hands and a shocked look on his face. The man he had been trying to help was gazing blankly at the sky.

She hung back, unable to do anything but stare as the paramedics rushed down the hill with the stretcher and did what they could to bring the man back to life. David answered the questions that he could, but she could tell that he was in shock.

They met the police in the parking lot. Detective Jefferson, the head detective at the Maple Creek Police Station, made a beeline for them after speaking with the paramedics.

"Why wasn't I surprised to hear your name mentioned in all of this?" he asked. "I was on my way out of the office, but I figured that I should take this. What happened? The paramedics told me that you found a man shot in the woods. Do you know anything else?"

"We heard the shot," Moira said. "It sounded close

by. I remember being surprised because I thought that the hunters could only hunt in the other part of the park. The screaming started a second later. We hurried forward and found the man. He was already unresponsive when we got there. David tried to stop the bleeding, but..." she trailed off. He knew what had happened after that. She looked over at her husband.

"David?" Detective Jefferson asked gently. "Do you have anything you'd like to add?"

Her husband shook his head. "I did everything I could," he said. "But it wasn't enough."

"I'm going to ask David to ride to the station with me," Jefferson said. "Not because he's in trouble, but because he's covered in blood and you probably don't want to get that all over your vehicle. Do you want to drop the dogs off at home, then meet us there?"

. . .

Moira had almost forgotten that the dogs were with them. She glanced down at Keeva and Maverick. The leashes were clenched in her hand. Both dogs seemed befuddled by all of the activity, and she felt a stab of guilt. She was glad that she had been holding onto their leashes; if she had left them tied up, she probably would have forgotten them completely.

"Okay," she said. "Are you okay with that, David?"

Her husband nodded. She tried to give him a reassuring smile, but it was hard with all of the blood on him.

She waited until he was in the back of the police car, then went over to the SUV. With a jolt, she realized that her keys were in the pocket of the bloodstained jacket that was now in the ambulance along with the man. Her car was locked, and there was no way she could open it, let alone start it. She had a spare set of keys at home, but would need David's house key to get them.

.   .   .

She ran forward and managed to wave down Detective Jefferson's car before he pulled out of the lot. After she explained the problem, he paged another officer and asked him to give her and the dogs a ride to her house. David handed her his set of keys, then she told him goodbye for a second time.

Shivering, she stood by her car with the dogs and waited. Hopefully the police vehicle would get there soon. Without her jacket, she was freezing.

As she stood there, she suddenly realized just how vulnerable she was. Whoever had shot the man was still out there. They might have done it by accident, but they still would probably want to hide their identity. What if the hunter came back to the parking lot and saw her there? She was glad she had the dogs with her. Anyone meaning to harm her would probably think twice about it with them there.

At last, she saw the police cruiser pull into the parking lot. The young officer was one that she didn't recognize. He had her put the dogs in the back seat, and let her ride in the front beside him.

"Where to, ma'am?" he asked.

She gave him her address, but had to direct him when they got closer. He parked in front of her house and waited while she put the dogs inside and grabbed a spare coat and an extra set of car keys. Feeling a bit better now that she had the dogs safe and had a new jacket on, she asked him if he'd been in touch with Detective Jefferson at all.

"No," he said. "He would call me if anything important had happened. I'm sure your husband is just fine. Ready to go see them?"

She nodded.

At the police station, she was directed to Detective Jefferson's office. David had gotten cleaned up, and had on a fresh shirt from one of the officers. He looked much better, and gave her a hug when she came in.

"Well, I think we have everything straightened out. I'll just need to take a statement from you, Moira, then the two of you can go. Someone will drive you back to the park so you can pick up your vehicle."

"Did they manage to resuscitate the man?" she asked.

"No," he said. "Unfortunately, it was too late. There wasn't anything that you could have done to help him, so I don't want you to feel bad about that."

"Do you have any idea who shot him?"

"Not yet. We recorded the license plate numbers of everyone who had parked in the parking lot, and we will be contacting everyone individually. We're also putting out a reward for any information that is offered up. My hope is that whoever did this will turn themselves in. If it was an accident, that would be the way to go."

"It's so frightening," Moira said. "It could have been one of us, or the dogs. How could it have been an accident? He was wearing orange."

"Unfortunately, some people are just too trigger-happy. They see movement, and then they fire. To be responsible while hunting means not firing until you have a clear line of sight on your target, but some people just get caught up in the moment. There will be serious consequences for whoever did this. Like I said, our hope is that they come forward themselves. If they don't, someone is bound to have some information."

Moira nodded. She was still shaken by what had happened, and she couldn't imagine what David must be feeling. She wished that they had been able to save the poor man. At least he hadn't been alone

49

at the end. She would just have to hope that he had taken some comfort in that.

After what seemed like hours, she pulled into their driveway. David had hardly said a word on the trip back to the park, and then back to the house. She turned off the engine.

"Are you going to be okay?" she asked him.

He nodded. "I'm just beating myself up. I keep thinking that if I had run faster, or if I had taken more first aid classes, I might have been able to save him."

"You heard what Detective Jefferson said. There was nothing we could have done."

"I know. But, it's just hard. I watched a man die in front of me. I had his blood on my hands."

. . .

"It's not your fault," she said. "Whoever shot him is the one who should be feeling like this, not you. Come on, let's go inside. We can start a fire, and I'll make some hot chocolate or warm apple cider. If you want to talk about it, we can, or we can just sit together."

He nodded. She gave his hand a squeeze, then opened the driver's side door. It hadn't exactly been the relaxing day off together that she had envisioned.

CHAPTER SIX

When Moira woke up Sunday morning, David was already awake and on his way out the door. He paused to give her a kiss and say goodbye, but she could tell that his mind was elsewhere. She didn't ask where he was going. He had his own way of processing things, and her guess was that he would be spending the day at the brewery, experimenting with new drafts or just cleaning and tending to his equipment. He found it relaxing, something that she could understand; she felt the same way about working in the deli.

She wasn't scheduled for that day, and she knew that her employees probably enjoyed having some time without her there, so she didn't want to go in on a day off and disturb them. She decided to turn her attention instead to Thanksgiving; it was less than a week away. She had already bought the essentials for the meal, and her fridge was full of food, as was her freezer. The turkey took up almost all of the room, in fact.

As she looked at the wealth of food in her fridge and freezer, she realized that she had probably outdone herself. Candice and Eli would be spending Thanksgiving on their own, in their new apartment. She didn't blame them; they were a young family, and wanted to do their own thing. Thanksgiving at her house would be just her, David, and Reggie, Eli's grandfather. As far as she was concerned, the more the merrier, especially on holidays. They had invited David's sister, Karissa, but she already had plans of her own.

Looking at the food in the fridge, she realized that they definitely had enough for more than just the three of them. Who else could she invite? The answer was obvious; Thelma and Allison. She wasn't sure if either of them had plans for the holiday, but it wouldn't hurt to ask.

She reached for her phone, then hesitated. She should probably ask David first, but she didn't want to bother him while he was trying to figure things out. She settled for sending him a text message.

A few minutes later, she got one back. "It's fine," he said. Something about the shortness of his reply made her wonder if it really was alright with him.

Should I call and ask him again? She wondered. She decided against it. She didn't want to bother him. If he really didn't want Thelma and Allison to come for Thanksgiving, he would have said so. He was an adult, after all, and he could say what he meant if it was important to him.

Still worried about her husband, she called Thelma. The older woman answered after a few rings. Moira got right to the point of her call.

. . .

"Would you and Allison like to come over for Thanksgiving dinner? It's just going to be David and me, and Eli's grandfather. Candice and Eli are doing their own thing for the holiday, and I have all of this extra food. I'd love it if you could come over."

"I'm not sure," Thelma said. "I'd love to, but Allison still hasn't told me what she wants to do for Thanksgiving. I mentioned spending it together, but she hasn't confirmed yet. If she is planning on it being just the two of us, I don't want to upset her."

"Do you mind if I ask her?" Moira said. "I should see her tomorrow at the deli."

"Go ahead, and let me know what she says. I just want her to be happy, the poor girl."

Moira said goodbye and ended the call, feeling even worse than she had before. Now she had both David and Allison to worry about. Both of them were struggling through their own problems, and neither wanted to talk about it.

"What's happening with the world?" she muttered.

Wanting the comfort of talking to someone who would understand, she dialed her daughter's number. It felt wonderful to hear Candice's voice.

"Hey, sweetie, how are you doing?" she said.

"Good. Busy, though. I've been working a lot. Eli is doing well. How are you guys?"

"I wish I could say good," Moira said. "Do you have some time to talk?"

"Of course. You have me worried now, Mom."

· · ·

"Sorry, sweetie," Moira said. "We're all fine, it's just a couple of things have happened recently."

She told her daughter about the man that she and David had found in the woods the day before. It was good to talk to someone about it. She wished that David would do the same with her. She was sure that he would feel better if he did.

"Oh my gosh, Mom, that's terrible," her daughter said. "I'm sorry. Maybe I should come back. I could just tell Eli that I want to have Thanksgiving with you guys..."

"No," Moira said. "You should do your own thing together if that is what you want. We'll be fine. I don't want you to worry about us, I just wanted someone to talk to."

"Do you know who he was?" her daughter asked. "The guy who died?"

· · ·

"Yes. His name was Norman Maines. I didn't know him personally, though."

"The name isn't familiar to me, thank goodness," her daughter said. "And everyone thinks it was a hunting accident?"

"That's what they're saying so far," Moira said.

"It kinda makes you wonder if it was on purpose, you know? If it was an accident, you would think whoever shot him would be frantic and try to get help."

"While that is something that you and I would try to do, I think there are quite a few people out there who would rather save their own skins if they did something like that. It's a sad truth about the world."

"I know," her daughter said, sighing. "Do you know anything about him other than his name?"

. . .

"I don't. I suppose I could look him up online," she said.

"It's not important, I'm just glad the two of you are okay. How's Allison doing?"

"She's still processing everything," Moira said. "I think it will just take her some time. Has she said anything to you?"

"Not for the past few days, but like I said, I've been pretty busy. She keeps beating herself up that she didn't know he was her father, but I keep telling her there is no way that she could have known. None of us knew."

Moira knew that emotions were rarely logical. She felt guilty about it as well; she had noticed the similarities between Allison and Candice back before Allison had even started working for her. In retrospect, she felt as if she should have guessed the truth, even though she knew that was ridiculous.

"I just feel like everything is falling apart," she said. "David's upset, Allison's upset, you live hours away, and I feel like I'm in a rut at the deli."

"Mom, that's ridiculous. The holidays are coming up, and you'll be busier than ever before you know it. Eli and I will be back for Christmas, and Allison just found out some pretty huge news. It'll take a while for her to get used to it. I'm sure David will come around in a day or two, and everything will be fine. Just take a deep breath and relax."

"Thanks," the Moira said with a wry smile. "Now that you mention it, I'll do just that, and I'm sure it will fix everything."

"I know it's easier said than done, but I've been trying not to worry about things I can't control. You should try the same thing. It's a good feeling."

. . .

"I'll try." "I love you, Candice. Thanks for talking. Tell Eli I say hi, I'm looking forward to seeing the two of you next month. I know that David is too."

"I will," Candice said. "I love you too, Mom. Bye."

Moira had just sat her phone down when it rang. Thinking it was Candice calling back, she answered it without checking the number. It took her a moment to realize that the person she was talking to was Allison, not her daughter.

"Ms. D., you should get to the deli right away," her employee said. "Someone just tried to break into the kitchen. I called the police and they will be here soon."

CHAPTER SEVEN

Moira rushed to the deli, her other problems forgotten in her desperation to see what damage had been done. Allison hadn't given her much information over the phone. She had been understandably upset, and Moira had been more concerned with getting to the scene of the crime than with pressing her for information. All she knew was that no one was hurt.

The deli's parking lot already had a pair of police vehicles in it when she pulled up. She got out of her car and hurried inside, coming face to face with Detective Jefferson.

. . .

"There you are," he said. "I knew you wouldn't be long."

"What happened?" she asked.

"Someone tried to break in through the side door," he said. "Your employees called the police right away. You are lucky that they hadn't opened for the day yet. I don't know what would have happened if whoever did this had been able to just walk in through the front door."

"Why would someone try to break in during the middle of the day?" she asked. "It doesn't make sense."

"I agree, it doesn't. I'm concerned that they may not have been here to rob the place. Their actions make me think that they were there to hurt someone."

The words chilled Moira. Who would want to hurt

one of her employees? She remembered the man dressed in black who had been there the week before. David was right; she should have told Jefferson immediately.

"Someone was here last week acting oddly," she said. "I saved the security footage from that morning. We can compare the tapes if the camera outside the side entrance caught them today."

With everything that had happened, she decided to keep the deli shut for the rest of the day. She locked the front doors, then she, her employees, and Detective Jefferson gathered to watch the security footage on her tablet. She brought up the footage from the week before and played it, pointing out the strange man to the detective. Then, she brought up this morning's footage. There was a single security camera outside the side entrance. Fortunately, it had caught the perpetrator on tape; unfortunately, there didn't seem to be any identifying features. The person was dressed in black, and was wearing a ski mask. From the angle of the camera, it was impossible to compare the person's height with the man who had visited the deli the week before.

"Do you happen to have the man's name?" Detective Jefferson asked.

"No," Moira said. "Unless Allison managed to get it. She was on shift when he was here."

The other woman shook her head. "Sorry, no. He only paid with cash, and he never mentioned his name."

The detective frowned. "Well, right now he is our only suspect," he said. "I'll take this footage and see what I can do. I'll also have a car patrol outside the deli for the next couple of days. If anything feels off, don't hesitate to give the station a call."

Moira thanked him for everything. Between the hunting accident victim and this, she had certainly taken up a lot of the police's time over the past few days. What was going on? Things really did seem to be falling apart. First Allison, then David, and now the deli? It seemed as if everything that could go wrong was doing so.

"The two of you should go home," she said to her employees. "Take the rest of the day off, and be careful. I'll be here first thing Monday morning, and I'll stick around all day in case anything else happens. Thank you so much for handling today. I'm sorry I wasn't here."

"It's fine, Ms. D.," Jenny said. "It was frightening, but I'm just glad that he didn't manage to get in. For once, I'm thankful that the door locks automatically."

Moira chuckled despite herself. They had all been locked out at one time or another by the side door. She was glad that it finally came to good use.

. . .

"Can I talk to you, Allison?" she asked as soon as Detective Jefferson left.

"Sure, what is it?" Allison asked.

"It's not about what happened today," Moira assured her. "It's about Thanksgiving. I was thinking of inviting you and your aunt over to my house for dinner with David, Reggie – that's Eli's grandfather – and me. I thought would be nice to do something together."

"Okay, that sounds nice, I guess," Allison said

"Okay, I'll clear that with your aunt. Go on and get some rest at home," she said. "Hopefully tomorrow will be better for all of us."

Alone in the deli, Moira realized that David had no idea what had happened. She called him, but he didn't answer. With a sigh, she left a message on his voicemail. She felt as if she was running out of people to turn to. Not only that, but everything she got involved in seemed doomed to suffer some sort of disaster. True, it hadn't been her fault that Candice's candy shop had burned down, but she had been married to Mike back when he had had the affair with Allison's mother. She should have known that something was going on. She should have had the sense to see what was wrong with their relationship back then, but she had been too blinded by love. And of course, yesterday it had been her idea to take that walk in the woods. If they had just stayed home, then David would never have had to watch a man die right in front of him.

And now, this. She should have told Detective Jefferson right away when that strange man had come into the deli. She hadn't, and now someone had almost broken in in broad daylight, and had terrified her employees. She couldn't help but wonder what would happen next. How was it that she couldn't seem to be able to do anything right anymore?

.   .   .

Frustrated, Moira sat down at the counter with her tablet, playing the security footage again. It didn't show anything new the second time around, or the third. She exited out of the program, wishing that she could do something to help fix at least one of the problems. Allison would have to come to terms with things in her own time, as would David. Maybe, however, she could do something about that poor man who had died. Candice was right; she should look up his name and see what he had been involved in. Maybe it was an accident after all, or maybe it was murder.

She typed the dead man's name into the search engine and waited as her Internet loaded the results. She was surprised when a couple of articles popped up. The man, it turned out, owned a small diner in Lake Marion. She herself had gone there a few times, along with her friends. She clicked on the top article. It was a news piece from the local paper about him selling the building. The photo featured him shaking hands with another man... a man whose face she knew very well.

CHAPTER EIGHT

Moira called Detective Jefferson with her discovery, assuring him that she definitely remembered the man's face. It was him. The same man. She had finally found the man who had been bothering her employees at the deli the week before. The article didn't give much information other than the man's name; Lance Vespers. The detective promised to look into it.

After getting off the phone with him, she shut off the tablet, but didn't get up. She didn't know what to do now. She didn't want to just sit at home alone with the dogs all day. She wanted to be active, to do something to help.

. . .

She decided to see if either of her two best friends were free. Both have been busy lately, Denise with her nephew, Logan, who had just gotten out of prison, and Martha with her boyfriend and her work. She decided to give her friends a call anyway. It was a Sunday afternoon; if there was a chance that either of them were free, it would likely be today.

She was rewarded when Denise told her that she was welcome to come over. "Bring Martha too," her friend said. "It's been a while since we've all been together."

It took some cajoling but after a while, Martha agreed to join them. Glad that she wasn't just going to go home and sit alone until David got back that evening, she slipped into the kitchen and packed up the remaining soup that would have just gone to waste otherwise. The three of them could have a nice lunch at Denise's house while she told them about everything that had happened.

. . .

While Moira and Denise had been friends for almost two years, Moira rarely went over to her friend's house. Denise, who spent much of her time managing the Redwood Grill, the busy upscale restaurant that she owned, seemed to appreciate her privacy. Moira could understand that; Denise was much busier than she was, and had to deal with ornery people all day at work. Compared to the Redwood Grill, Darling's Delicious Delights was a quiet, relaxing workplace.

Moira pulled up her friend's driveway and parked in front of the house. She lifted the bag of warm soup she had packed into multiple to-go containers and slipped the strap of her purse over her shoulder. She realized with a jolt that Logan would be there. She hadn't seen her ex-employee since he had been arrested. Suddenly spending the afternoon with her friends was beginning to look a lot less relaxing.

Stalling, she checked her phone one last time. David still hadn't called her back. She knew he was probably just busy doing things at the brewery, but she couldn't help but worry about him. Maybe Denise would have a good solution. She had had her own fair share of experiences with relationship troubles.

Lifting her two bags, she got out of the car and pushed the door shut with her hip. Not bothering to lock it, she walked up to the porch. She managed to knock on the door with her hands full, and a moment later, Denise answered.

"Come on in," her friend said. "Do you need me to take something?"

"I've got it," Moira said.

She followed her friend through the house to the kitchen, where she put down the heavy bag full of soup containers.

"What is today's special?" Denise asked.

· · ·

"Broccoli cheddar soup," she said.

"Why do you have so much of it?" Denise asked, peering into the bag. "I don't think we will be able to eat all of this."

"That is partially why I am here," Moira said. "There's something I have to tell you."

"Did something happen? Is the deli all right?"

"Let's wait until Martha gets here," Moira said. "I don't want to have to repeat myself too much. Everyone is fine, though." She frowned. Well, not everyone. The poor man they had found in the woods was dead.

"How long did she say she would be?"

"She should be here soon," Moira said. "She said she

said a couple of things to finish up at home before heading over. It's good to see you again. It's been a while since we've had lunch together."

"I know. This will be nice... depending on your news, I suppose. Everyone's really okay?"

"David and I are fine," she said. "The deli is fine. Someone did —"

She broke off as a young man walked into the kitchen. She hadn't seen Logan for months, and he had changed quite a bit since then. He had a scruffy beard, and was even thinner than before. He froze when he saw her.

"Sorry, I didn't know..."

He began to back out of the kitchen. Denise stepped forward and grabbed his arm. "Logan, get in here. You can't avoid Moira forever."

"I doubt she wants to see me," he muttered. "I'll just go back into my room."

Denise let him go and put her hands on her hips. "You have done nothing but hide in your room since you got back. I've been trying to be understanding, but this is ridiculous. You can't spend the rest of your life hiding from the world. If you won't say hi to Moira, who is the nicest person in the world, then maybe I should kick you out and force you to start interacting with people. I fought for months to give you your life back. Don't you dare waste it. What would your mother think?"

Logan stared at his aunt with wide eyes. Moira didn't blame him; she was glad that Denise's outburst hadn't been directed toward her.

"Sorry," he mumbled. "Hi, Ms. D."

. . .

"Hi, Logan," she replied. "How are you doing?"

"Better, now that... well, it's good to be home."

She nodded, understanding that he didn't want to mention his stay in prison. She was glad to avoid the subject as well. He had killed a troubled man in self-defense, but the case had been complicated and she still wasn't sure how she felt about everything. Still, she was glad that Denise had managed to appeal his case and get him home. The Logan that she knew was a good kid, and didn't deserve to spend years behind bars.

"It's good to see you again," she said.

"You too." He looked at his aunt. "Um, well, I'm just going to grab a snack and then head back to my room, if that's okay with you."

. . .

"Take a cup of soup if you'd like," Moira said. "Or a couple. It's broccoli cheddar. We've got plenty."

She saw the ghost of a smile on his face. "Thanks," he said. "I will."

Martha arrived not long after Logan vanished back into his room. The three of them sat around Denise's kitchen table. None of them reached for the soup; the two women stared at Moira eagerly, waiting for her to spill the beans.

"Well, there are a few things," she began. "This might take a while..."

Once she was done telling them everything that had happened over the past few days, the kitchen fell silent. After a moment, Denise said, "Well, you certainly don't have a quiet life. I'm glad you and David are okay. It's scary to think someone got shot in the woods not far from where you were walking."

· · ·

"I know," Moira said. "I'm just so grateful that it wasn't one of us that got hit."

"Do you think it was really an accident?" Martha asked.

"I have no idea. All I know about the guy is that he was selling his restaurant, but I can't see how that would be a motive for murder."

"Didn't you say the guy he was selling it to is the same one who tried to break into the deli?"

"To be fair, I'm not completely sure he's the one who tried to break in." She sighed. "But who else could it be?"

"Do you think the hunter's death and the break-in at the deli are related?" Denise asked.

. . .

"I... I don't know." Moira frowned. Everything had happened so quickly. She had only gotten the news about the deli a couple of hours ago. "I don't see how the crimes could be tied together. I didn't know the man who got shot, and the deli has no connections to his diner. The only thing linking the crimes is that man, Lance. I still don't know what his interest in the deli was."

"That's not the only thing that ties them together," her friend said. When Moira looked at her blankly, Denise continued, "You. You own the deli, and you're also the one who found the hunter in the woods. I know it seems like a stretch, but maybe that has something to do with it."

The deli owner bit her lip. Denise was right. What if she had been looking at everything wrong? She had thought the two incidents were unrelated, but what if they weren't? If whoever had killed the hunter knew that she had found the body, then maybe the attack on the deli had been a warning or, even worse, an attempt on her life.

CHAPTER NINE

After their impromptu lunch together, Moira gave her friends a warm goodbye before getting back into her car. While it warmed up, she considered what she wanted to do next. She could go home, but with the house empty and so much on her mind, she knew that she wouldn't be able to relax. The deli was closed for the day while the police looked into the break-in attempt, and David was at the brewery. She could go and spend some time there, but she wanted to respect his need for space.

I just wish I knew if the hunter's death and the issues at the deli are related, she thought. She didn't know if she and the people she loved were in danger. A simple break-in attempt was bad enough, but what if the perpetrator hadn't been after money? What if he or she had been trying to send her a message?

If that was the case, then maybe she really should just go and sit at home. She didn't want to endanger the people she cared about by snooping around when someone wanted her to go away.

Just as she put the car into gear, having decided that it might be best to play it safe, her phone rang. She was relieved to see David's name on her screen. Putting her car back into park, she took the call.

"Hey," she said. "Are you okay?"

"I should be asking you that," her husband said. "I got your message. Is everyone all right? Do they have a suspect in custody yet?"

· · ·

"Everyone is fine. They don't have anyone in custody yet, but they do have a suspect."

"Are you home? I'm on the way over."

"I'm at Denise's," she said, "I was just about to leave."

"I'm sorry. I shouldn't have gone to the brewery this morning and should have been there when you got the call about the deli."

"Neither of us could have known," she said. "It's okay. Like I said, no one got hurt."

"I still feel bad. Do you want to get lunch somewhere?"

She hesitated. "I'm sorry, I just ate with Denise and Martha. I still have some leftover soup if you're hungry. If you just want to get coffee, we could meet at that little coffee shop in Lake Marion."

"Sure," he said. "I need to stop at the office anyway. I'll just lock up here and then head over. I love you."

"I love you too," Moira said. She ended the call, feeling better than she had just a few minutes ago.

At least David seemed to be doing all right. She knew that they still had a lot to talk about. Seeing someone die right in front of you, someone that you are struggling to save, couldn't be easy.

She drove toward Lake Marion, finding it hard to believe that Thanksgiving was in just a few days. She didn't feel like she was in the holiday spirit at all. Usually, she loved Thanksgiving; it was a time to go all out with cooking, have family and friends over, and enjoy being together. Now, she had so much to worry about. Allison, David, the murder, the attack on the deli; nothing was going right. She had a feeling that things would continue to get worse until whoever was behind the attack was stopped.

Now that it had been mentioned, she was unable to shake the suspicion that the attempted break-in at the deli and the attack on the hunter in the woods were somehow related. She just didn't understand why. Lance was the one who she thought had most likely tried to break into the deli, but he didn't make sense as a suspect for the hunter's death. He had been buying the man's diner, after all.

She frowned. In fact, maybe his interest in buying a restaurant had something to do with why he had been snooping around the deli. She knew her deli was one of the most well-known restaurants in the area. If he was interested in being competitive, he very well might have just been curious to see how they did things. If he had asked her, she would have been happy to give him a tour and some advice, but she knew that most places probably wouldn't have welcomed competition with open arms.

. . .

She knew that the reality was probably that there was no connection between the two crimes. The man who died in the woods could have truly been the victim of a hunting accident, and the attempted break-in at the deli could have simply been some misguided low-level criminal's attempts to rob them.

All she had were suspicions, guesses, and the gut feeling that there was more going on than met the eye. None of those things would hold up in court, and none of them would be enough to give Detective Jefferson a good reason to think the crimes were linked.

The coffee shop was on the corner of Lake Marion's main street and the road that curved around the lake that the town was named after. The lake itself was a cold, steel blue color. Waves lapped at the shore, and the beaches were empty. It would be a good six months or more before anyone went swimming in the waters again.

The diner that Lance was buying from Norman

Maines was only a few buildings away from the coffee shop. Moira hadn't chosen this intentionally when she had made plans with her husband, but as she pulled past the building, she still felt a little stab of guilt. She had just decided to stay out of things to keep herself and her employees and family safe, but here she was, just a few hundred feet away from the building that – if her wild guesses were right – was the reason for a murder. She still didn't understand what possible motivation the killer could have had, but there had to be a connection. The two towns were small, but she still thought that it was quite a coincidence that she had seen Lance the week before the man had been killed in the woods. That, plus the break-in attempt, was just too much of a coincidence to ignore.

Figuring that she was already there, and the damage had already been done, she parked her SUV along the road instead of in the coffee shop's small parking lot so she could keep an eye on the diner. She wasn't surprised to see that the doors were closed and the normally glowing open sign was off. The restaurant's owner was dead, and it seemed that the sale hadn't gone through yet. The employees were probably in mourning, and the future of the restaurant would be uncertain.

She realized with the chill that if she had been the one to get hit by a stray bullet, then it would be the deli that would be dark and empty as her own employees mourned her passing.

She saw David's vehicle coming down the road toward her. He pulled into the parking lot, and she got out of her SUV. He pulled her into a hug when she got close enough.

"Are you sure you're okay?"

"I wasn't even there when it happened," she said. "I'm fine. Everyone else is fine too. The side door is a little bit dented, but that's it."

"When I find out who did it..."

· · ·

"I'll press charges," she said. "Whoever tried to break in terrified Allison and Jenny. I'm not going to let that slide."

"I know you won't," he said, giving her a kiss. "I love how protective you are of your employees. Come on, let's go in. It's cold out here."

They ordered their coffees and sat at a small table in the corner. Moira wrapped her hands around the warm cup. It was nice spending some time with David, even if they both had a lot on their minds.

"How are you doing?" she asked. "After what happened yesterday, if there's anything you want to talk about, you know I'm here for you."

"I know," he said. "I'm sorry. I should have stuck around for longer this morning. I just didn't feel like I was ready to discuss anything. I know what you're going to say; that it's not my fault, that I did everything I could to save him... and I know you're right. But that doesn't change how terrible I feel about it."

"I'm sorry," she said. "You're right, that is exactly what I would've said, and it's true. But I also know how much of a disconnect there can be between what you know in your mind, and what you feel in your heart. It can be difficult to make your emotions line up with logic."

"I've seen a lot of terrible things in my job," he said. "And I've lost friends, but somehow, this was worse."

"Did he say anything before he passed away?" she asked.

"No, he didn't. He just stared up at me, and I saw the look in his eyes. He thought I was going to help him. He thought I was going to save him, and I let him down. And now I just keep thinking about how he will never have Thanksgiving with his family again, or watch his grandchildren open their Christmas presents. He will never see spring come, or go fishing, or even sit down and drink a cup of coffee like we are now."

"They'll find whoever shot him," she said. "I know they will. There were only a few cars parked in the lot. They can trace the license plates, and bring every single person in for questioning. Someone must have seen something."

"Between that and what happened at the deli, I'm beginning to feel like I can't keep anyone safe. I should've been there for you today. It makes me so angry that someone tried to break into your restaurant."

"I know," Moira said with feeling. "Trust me, I feel the same. After this, I think I'm going to go home and call Detective Jefferson and see if he's made any progress yet. Then, I'll go over the security footage again. I also need to figure out what I'm going to do for security at the deli until the person who did this is caught. I can't risk that person

PATTI BENNING

coming back and actually hurting one of my
employees this time."

If that happened, she didn't know if she would ever
forgive herself. Keeping the people she cared about
safe was more important than making money, and
she would keep the deli closed until the culprit was
caught if she had to.

CHAPTER TEN

They finished their coffees together, then Moira remembered what David had said about needing to stop at his office. "What do you need to get at the office?" she asked.

"I've got an interview scheduled with a client Friday morning," her husband said. "I've seen him before, and I just want to pick up the files from the previous case so I can look them over."

"I'll go with you," Moira said. "I wanted to pick up Maverick's dog bed and wash the cover."

. . .

She loved David's office. It was comfortable and felt like home, almost as much as her own house did. The furniture was perfectly worn and more comfortable than her own couch at home. The decor was so perfectly David, that she could hardly imagine the building having ever belonged to anyone else.

They walked in together, Moira putting her purse down and David tossing his keys onto his desk. "I hope things start to pick up again soon here," she said. "It's been so slow lately."

"People are just busy with the holidays," he said. "There are usually a few more cases around Christmas. Something about the Christmas season makes some people go off the edge. Then, of course, around Valentine's Day, I will be getting a slew of adultery cases."

Moira smiled. She knew that her husband always regarded the adultery cases with caution. Some of his worst clients had come from them, not to mention the clients that he had simply had to cut off.

He always felt bad taking money from people he couldn't help, and some people were just determined to be jealous even when nothing was going on. She was glad that she and David had a different sort of relationship. They trusted each other, and that was important.

"I'm glad you kept this business open," she said, relaxing in the comfortable chair behind his desk as he dug through the file cabinet. "I love this place. I know it takes up a lot of your time, but I'd be sad if you shut it down."

"I have considered closing the doors for good," he admitted. "But the truth is, I'm always drawn back to this line of work. It's a good excuse to get out and about, instead of sitting locked up in the brewery all day. I suppose that this job has become sort of a hobby that acts as a break from my other hobby, which has become my actual full-time job."

Moira chuckled at that. "It's amazing how life changes, isn't it? Some changes are all at once, and others are so gradual that you hardly realize they are happening."

She got off the chair and knelt on the floor, unzipping the dog bed's cover so she could take it home. It certainly needed a good wash. She was beginning to pull it off the bed itself when someone knocked at the door. She and David exchanged a look.

"Well, your car is parked out front," she said. "I suppose someone thinks this place is open."

"I'll see who it is," David said. "You're right, it has been pretty slow. I guess I should take cases where I can find them."

She continued pulling out the dog bed while David spoke to whoever was out front. She heard the front door shut, and two sets of footsteps coming back. She straightened up, making sure the place looked presentable. When she saw who was with her husband, she froze.

.   .   .

It was Lance. The other man was wearing all black again, but this time without the hat. He seemed as shocked to see her as she was to see him.

"I didn't know you were with a client already," he said.

"This is my wife, Moira Darling," David said. "She works with me sometimes. Come on in and sit down. Like I said, I was just stopping by to pick up some papers, but I've got time to talk to you about your case for a few minutes."

"David... can I talk to you?" Moira asked.

Her husband raised his eyebrows. "Of course. I'm sorry, Mr. Vespers, you can take a seat. This will be just a second."

.   .   .

She and David walked into the hallway. Lowering her voice, she said, "That's him. That is Lance, the guy I was telling you about. The one who was taking photos of the deli."

David frowned. "What do you want me to do? We should figure out why he's here, at least."

"You're right... I guess..." she hesitated. "I guess just treat him like a normal client. Maybe we'll find out something about him when he tells us what he wants."

"Okay. Do you want to come back in, or do you think it's best if I do this on my own?"

"I want to hear everything he says."

Her husband hesitated, then nodded. "Okay."

. . .

They returned to the office. Lance was seated in a chair, but stood up as they came in. "If this isn't a good time, I can come back later."

"No," David said. "This is fine. It won't take long. All I will do right now is figure out if I can help you. We can talk more later."

"All right," he said. He glanced at Moira, then sat back down. "So, my problem is this. Someone I was about to enter into a business deal with was killed. I was just taken down to the police station for questioning. I know you're not a lawyer, and that's not what I'm looking for. I already have my own lawyer working on my case. My problem is that I am still planning on buying the restaurant, so if someone has an issue with the place, I want to know who it is. I want to know what I'm getting into before it's too late."

"Are you still buying the restaurant even though the owner is dead?" Moira asked.

. . .

"We had already signed everything," Lance said. "All that was left was for me to pick up the keys. I'm sure there'll be some sort of delay while everything is investigated, but yes, I'm still planning on buying it." He hesitated, then said, "I'm sorry if I bothered you at the deli last week. I wasn't trying to upset your employees. I just wanted to see how things worked, and to get a feel for what I was up against – not that I'm trying to steal your business. I'm new to all of this, and just wanted to take a look at a successful local business before jumping headfirst into my own."

Moira considered what he had said. She couldn't tell if he was a good liar, or he was really telling the truth. Even though she was still undecided about him, she nodded and said "I understand. Next time, you can just call me and ask me for a tour. I'm happy to help people out. I know how stressful it can be to enter the restaurant industry as a newcomer."

"Thank you. I may take you up on that offer."

. . .

"So, you want me to look into the diner's history, and find any people who might have had a problem with it or with the owner?" David said, bringing them back to the reason for Lance's visit.

"Yes. And, of course, if you happen to find something that can be admissible in a courtroom that would perhaps exonerate me, that would be a bonus." He gave a dry chuckle. "I don't know if I can go back on the sale now anyway, but if I'm about to enter into some major family drama or a lawsuit waiting to happen, I want to know about it beforehand."

David nodded. "That's understandable, and it sounds like something we could help you with. I charge by the hour, with a fifty-percent retainer up front. We can discuss your budget, and I won't go over it without talking to you."

"That sounds good to me. When do you think you might have something by?"

. . .

"I don't know. I'll do what I can before Thanksgiving, but I am taking Thursday off to be with my family. I'm not sure how long it will take to turn something up, or if there is even anything to find in the first place. In the meantime, I'd suggest just keeping your eyes and ears peeled, and don't meet with anyone alone until you have some answers."

CHAPTER ELEVEN

On Thanksgiving morning, Moira woke up to the sound of gobbling turkeys. She sat bolt upright in bed, blinking in the morning light. Beside her, David chuckled and shut off his phone, on which the recording of turkeys had been playing.

"You said not to let you sleep in too late," he said, laughing as she threw a pillow at him.

"I didn't mean for you to wake me up by giving me a heart attack."

. . .

"It was supposed to get you into the holiday spirit," he said. "It's the big day."

"You're in a good mood," she grumbled. She wasn't really angry, but she didn't want to encourage him. What would he do to wake her up on Christmas, go stomp around on the roof in boots?

"I think taking Lance's case was good for me. It's giving me a way to focus my energy, instead of dwelling on what happened."

"What if he's the killer? I don't like you meeting with him alone."

"I don't think he is. He seems genuinely concerned about his associate's death, and is spending quite a bit of money to get it figured out."

"He could just be trying to make himself look innocent," she said.

. . .

"True, but he would have to be betting on me not finding out the truth. I know my focus hasn't been on the investigative business recently, but I still have a pretty good reputation."

She sighed, dropping the argument. They had had the same one every morning since he had taken the case on Sunday. She didn't like Lance, though she knew she was probably biased. She would just have to trust her husband's judgment. It had been pretty good so far.

"Shoot, I have to put the turkey in," she said, glancing at the clock. "It's going to take hours to cook."

"Let me help you."

"I don't need help with the turkey, but could you do me a favor and make sure the outside of the house looks nice? I don't want to risk Reggie slipping on any damp leaves, and besides, Thelma has never seen the place."

"Sure. What do you want to do about breakfast? Do you want me to make something while you work on the turkey?"

She bit her lip. "No, let's just eat cereal. I don't want to start off the day with a sink full of dirty dishes. Besides, we shouldn't eat too much now. I want everyone to be nice and hungry for the meal this afternoon."

Their tasks determined, she went downstairs and put the dogs out back before washing her hands and pulling the enormous turkey out of the refrigerator.

Setting it on the counter, she pulled out the spices that she would mix together for her special dry rub. She had made it the same way since Candice was a young child, and was looking forward to eating it that afternoon. After the craziness of the past week, she couldn't think of anything more comforting than a good, old-fashioned roasted turkey.

After rubbing the turkey, she put it in the oven. Every couple of hours she would check it, taking the temperature with a meat thermometer and basting it to keep it moist. She would stuff it after it came out, and before she presented it to the table.

With the turkey in the oven, she had fulfilled her cooking duties for the moment, but there was still a lot to do. She let the dogs back inside, then went into the basement to find the extra leaf for their table. She also brought up one of the fancier tablecloths, which would replace their usual one with the flower pattern.

Once the table was set, she began cleaning the rest of the house. With Reggie arriving soon, she wanted the bulk of the cleaning to be done ahead of time.

. . .

An hour later, she returned to the kitchen, already feeling exhausted. She had worked like a whirlwind, and had managed to vacuum the living room, sweep the rest of the floors, and clean the windows. The dogs had been locked behind the gate to the mudroom. Despite their comfortable beds, toys, and full bowl of water, they were moping.

"It's just until everyone's here and settled," she said. "I don't want you to knock Reggie over when he comes in. Shoot. Actually, I should get going now to go get him."

She found David out front, finishing up sweeping the rest of the leaves off the porch.

"Are you on your way out?" he asked.

"Yep," she said. "Can you do me a favor and check on the turkey in about an hour if I am not back? I don't want it to dry out."

. . .

"Of course. Is there anything else you need me to do?"

"I don't think so. Just tidy up anything that you think needs it, and make sure the dogs are behind the gate. If you want to get some drinks ready for when Reggie gets here, you could do that."

"Okay." He paused in his sweeping to give her a kiss. "I'll see you soon. Drive safely."

She pulled out of the driveway and turned toward Lake Marion, hardly concentrating as she took the familiar roads. Oddly enough, she did feel better today. She was still worried about what had happened, but she decided to keep it out of her mind for the day. Today was about focusing on being with her friends and family, and everything that they had to be thankful for, and if she was being honest with herself, she really did have a lot to be thankful for. She had the best husband in the world, and a wonderful daughter. Her daughter had a good husband of her own, and was pursuing a career in something that she enjoyed. She also had two pampered dogs, her best friends, and, of course, the deli.

All in all, she was a lucky person. Bad things would always happen, no matter how hard she tried to prevent them. She knew that she should try to start focusing on the good things, like Candice had said, instead of those things that she had no control over.

She pulled into the assisted living home's parking lot. It was packed. Not wanting to make Reggie walk across the parking lot, she pulled up in front of the front doors. She hoped he would be ready to go, so she wouldn't have to sit there long. It was technically an ambulance lane, but people often used it to pick up and drop off their loved ones.

She went inside and found herself in an envelope of warm air that smelled like food and cleaner. Thanksgiving and Christmas were the two busiest days of the year for the assisted living home, when people came to visit their families and eat dinner with them. She looked around, but didn't see Reggie. She tracked down one of the staff, and found out that he was in his room.

A few minutes later, she knocked on his door. He called out to her to come in, which she did. "Oh, you're here already? I must have lost track of the time. I'm just about ready to go, I just need to put my shoes and jacket on."

"Here, let me help you with that," she said, grabbing his jacket for him. "It's chilly outside."

"I know. I saw the snow last night. It all melted this morning, but it won't be long until it sticks around."

"I'm glad you're coming to dinner, Reggie," she said. "It will be nice to have you there."

"Thank you for inviting me. I'm looking forward to

your food. You're such a wonderful cook. Nothing compares to a homemade turkey dinner."

"I hope it's good," she said. "I still have a lot of work to do, so we should get going."

She helped him down the hall to the office, where he checked out. She was glad to see him smile and joke around with the staff member. It seemed like a good place for him to be, and he had never complained about the people there. She still felt bad that he hadn't been able to move in with Candice and Eli like he had been planning to, but he had taken it all in stride.

"Are you ready?" she asked.

"Let's get out of here."

She helped him into the car, then pulled out of the parking lot. It felt good to be on the road again, and out of the busy building. She drove back to town, slowing slightly in front of the diner. It was closed, and she wondered whether it would ever reopen. Would Lance really buy it? Even if he did, would he have what it took to keep it from failing?

She hesitated as she saw the woman who lived next door to the diner raking leaves outside. She recognized Jeanie, the waitress that had served her and David on Saturday. If anyone knew what was going on with the restaurant, it would be her. The older woman had worked there for thirty years, and would have all the answers that Moira wanted.

"Do you mind if I stop and talk to this woman for a second?" she asked Reggie. "I'll be quick, I promise."

"You do whatever you want," he said. "I'm just going to enjoy the scenery. It's been a while since I've gotten out of there."

She pulled up along the curb and rolled down the

window. "Hi," she called out. "Sorry to bother you, but I was wondering if I could talk to you for a second?"

The other woman squinted at her. "You own the deli, don't you?"

"Yes. It's me, Moira Darling. I just want to ask you something about the diner. I know it's a holiday, so if you want me to go away, just say so. I don't want to disturb you."

"I'm not doing anything today. My family is all out of state, and doesn't make sense to make a big dinner for myself. If you want to come in for a minute, that's fine."

Moira told Reggie she would be right out. Leaving the keys with him, she went inside. It was time to finally get some answers.

CHAPTER TWELVE

"Come on in, I was just about to take a break anyway," the other woman said. "My fingers are getting cold. I really should be wearing gloves."

"I don't need to talk long. I feel bad for interrupting you, but I didn't know when I would see you again. I just wanted to ask you about the diner."

"It's already sold, if that's what you're thinking," the other woman said, making a face. "Old Mr. Maines sold it before he kicked the bucket." Moira winced. The way she referred to the other man's death made her uncomfortable.

. . .

"I know. I was just wondering if you knew if there was anyone who might have had it out for him?"

The other woman raised her eyebrows. "Everyone liked him," she said. "The diner's been here for decades. If you're getting at someone killing him, I think that's pretty unlikely."

"How was his relationship with Lance Vespers?"

"The buyer? As far as I know, the two of them hit it off well. He didn't try to short him on the price at all, and paid what he was asking. The sale took all of two meetings before they finalized things."

Moira frowned. The more she heard about him, the less likely she thought it was that Lance had killed the other man. He would simply have had no motive... unless he had decided to back out of the sale, and couldn't. Was that why he had hired David? To find out if there was anything about the diner's history that might void the sale?

"Is there any reason you can think of that Lance might have wanted to back out of buying it?"

"I don't think so," the other woman said. "He seemed pretty happy with it."

"I see." She felt deflated. Every theory she had seemed to be wrong.

"I get why you're asking these questions," the other woman said. "You know Lance, don't you? I didn't like him much either. There's just something about him that rubs you wrong, isn't there?"

The deli owner nodded. "He stopped into Darling's Delicious Delights last week, and was snooping around, taking pictures and trying to look into the kitchen. He made my employees uncomfortable, and he made me uncomfortable too."

"I heard about the break-in at your place. It was in the newspaper. It's so odd, isn't it? I wonder what he's playing at."

Moira blinked. Jeanie seemed to have come full circle; just moments before, she had been saying how she didn't think Lance had any reason to kill Norman Maines, but now it sounded like she thought he might have had something to do with the break-in at the deli.

"Are you saying he had something to do with what happened at my restaurant?"

"I don't know. What do you think?" The woman's eyes seemed to brighten as she continued. "You know, now that you think about it, I did find him pretty suspicious. I sure hope the police consider him a suspect."

. . .

"They do," Moira said. "I know he has a lawyer, but I'm not sure how the case is going."

"I wonder what will happen to the diner if he gets convicted," the other woman said.

"I have no idea," Moira said. "I don't know enough about legal stuff to know whether or not the sale would be canceled, or anything like that. From what I heard, he had done everything except pick up the keys. It sounded like finishing the process would be quite a mess either way."

"I hope he doesn't get the diner," the other woman said heatedly.

Surprised that the emotion her voice, Moira said, "Why?"

. . .

"I know Lance liked him, but I think he was just glad for the quick sale. I don't think he would be the kind of owner that the diner would need. He wants to change almost everything right away, when he takes control of the place. He said that he would be hiring a whole new team of employees." She gave a bitter laugh. "As if it's our fault that the diner is going downhill. We were the only ones keeping it afloat. Now, I've been working there for thirty years. You would think he would listen to me, but no." Looking embarrassed at her own outburst, the other woman began to backpedal. "Of course, he probably wouldn't really fire all of us. He would need some people to show him how it's done, and besides, I should retire anyway. I really wish I could start my own restaurant. I wanted to try to get the money together to buy the diner, but Mr. Maines didn't want to wait."

"I'm sorry. It sounds like a difficult situation for everyone. Thank you for answering my questions. I'm sorry for taking up so much of your time. I've got a Thanksgiving dinner to cook now, so I should be getting home."

. . .

"I was glad to talk to someone. There's not much that gets me angry, but the diner is like my second home, and I would hate to see it driven into the ground."

The other woman walked her out, leading her toward the front door. Moira's gaze wandered as she tried to process everything she had just learned. It sounded like lots of people had good reason to want to kill Lance, but no one had a good reason to want to kill Norman. If Lance was innocent, then who had done it? Who had pulled the trigger?

As if on cue, her eyes landed on a rifle in the corner by the front door. Hanging next to it was a camouflage jacket. It looked like Jeanie was a hunter.

CHAPTER THIRTEEN

"Is everything all right?" the other woman asked.

Moira tore her gaze away from the gun, but saw that it was already too late. Jeanie was looking between the rifle and her, an expression of dawning realization on her face. The look was unmistakable. She had been caught.

Stiffly, she reached for the gun. "I should have put that away, but I didn't know I would be having a visitor."

.   .   .

"There's nothing wrong with hunting," Moira said, trying to sound casual.

The other woman stared at her for a long moment. Moira stared back, trying to keep her face neutral, but knew she was failing. Her heart was pounding at what felt like a million beats per minute in her chest.

"You're going to call the police, aren't you? You're a smart woman. I said too much. You made the connection."

The deli owner closed her eyes. It was true. They were at an impasse. "Did you kill him?" she asked.

"Why would I tell you?" the other woman said coldly.

"I never once considered you," she said, taking the woman's lack of denial as an affirmation. "I guess, looking back, I should have. Are you the one that

THANKSGIVING DELI MURDER

tried to break into the deli, too, or was that really Lance?"

The other woman hesitated. Moira continued, "Look, I already know you killed someone. I just want to know that my employees won't be in danger anymore."

"I was trying to send a message," Jeanie said. "I didn't want to hurt anyone. Right after I shot my boss, I saw you and your husband through the trees, and I realized who you were. You have a reputation around town. I thought that by frightening you, I might make you think twice about nosing into this case."

"How far were you going to take it?" Moira asked. "How far would you go to cover up your crime?"

"As soon as I heard that Lance was a suspect, I stopped," the other woman said. "I didn't want to hurt anyone other than Mr. Maines, and maybe

127

Lance, that's all. All I wanted was to stop the sale of the diner."

"By committing murder?" the deli owner asked. "That's not the answer."

"I didn't plan it, if that's what you're thinking," the other woman said. "I was out in the woods, looking for a good spot to sit for a couple of hours, and I saw him sitting on a log talking on his cell phone. He was talking about the sale, for goodness sake. Not only was he selling the place I had worked at for thirty years to someone who was planning on firing the entire staff, but he was also scaring away my deer. Something inside me just snapped. I figured no one would ever know."

The deli owner shivered. She could understand how upset the other woman must have been, but the fact that she would actually take that step to become a killer was frightening. No matter how much Moira loved the deli, she would never kill to protect it.

People were always so much more important than business and money.

"I'm sure you wish you could go back and undo it," she said. "Now, are you going to put the gun down?"

"I... I don't want to go to jail," the woman said. She hesitated, and Moira saw the gun's barrel drop. Then it rose again, this time pointing decisively at her chest. "I already killed to protect my job. I think I will be okay with killing to protect my freedom."

She clicked the safety off. The deli owner put her hands up, taking a step back.

"Please, just think before you..."

The gun went off. Moira's ears rang and she heard the sound of breaking glass faintly. She stumbled backward, waiting for the pain to hit her, but it never came.

. . .

Moira opened her eyes, wondering how the woman had missed such a close shot. She saw that she was shaking like a leaf, and was barely able to hold the gun straight. No matter what she had said, committing a second murder seemed to be harder than she had expected.

While she struggled to rack another round into the chamber, Moira realized that this was her chance. If she was going to save herself, it had to be now. She turned and took off down the hallway, not pausing to look behind her. She skidded to a halt in the kitchen, looking around for a back exit, but not finding one. She took the only door she could see. It led to the basement.

Leaving the lights off, she went downstairs and shut the door behind her quietly, hearing the other woman's footsteps rushing down the hall. She inched down the stairs, feeling around herself in the dark. She managed to squeeze into a small spot beneath the staircase, but without any source of light, it was difficult to tell how hidden she was.

. . .

The basement light clicked on. Jeanie took the stairs slowly. There was just enough light for Moira to see the outlines of the boxes surrounding her. If the other woman came around far enough, she would be able to see her easily. Even worse, she was trapped. There was no way out without exposing herself to the woman's rifle.

Holding her breath and trying her best to be silent, Moira looked into the closest open box. There was nothing she could use as a weapon, other than a small bowl with some loose marbles in it. That gave her an idea. She took a few into her hand, then settled back into her nook under the staircase.

Her heart hammering, she waited as the other woman came even closer. One more step, and she would see Moira. Taking careful aim, Moira tossed one of the marbles between the steps. It hit a box on the other side of the basement. The other woman spun around and hurried back in that direction. Moira breathed a sigh of relief, knowing that she had only bought herself a few seconds, but it was better than nothing.

. . .

If only she could make it upstairs before the other woman got a chance to get a shot off, and she might be able to lock her in the basement. She began to inch her way out of the hiding spot. Her foot bumped a box that was lighter than she expected, and she froze as it shifted. However, at that exact moment, sirens began to wail in the distance. The sound covered up any noise she might have made, and the other woman rushed upstairs.

Moira waited only a few seconds before going up the stairs herself. She heard shouting at the front door, and another gunshot went off. She wanted desperately to help, but didn't know if the sudden appearance of another woman would confuse matters, and she also didn't want to put herself in the path of any stray bullets.

In the next room, she found the back door that she had been looking for. She went outside and hurried around the side of the house, coming face to face with a young police officer.

· · ·

"Don't shoot," she said, throwing her hands up. "That woman tried to kill me. My name is Moira Darling. I own the deli in Maple Creek."

"Moira?" the officer said. She recognized him as the one who had driven her home from the park. She breathed a sigh of relief.

"Yes, it's me. She's the one that tried to break into the deli, and she's the one that shot the man in the woods."

"All right, come with me. I'll keep you safe. Your friend Reggie is the one who called us. He might've saved your life."

Relieved, she followed him around to the front of the building, where she saw Jeanie in handcuffs. Somehow, the police had managed to subdue her without any casualties, and as the deli owner watched, she was loaded into the back of a police car. Moira breathed a sigh of relief. She knew that it was only thanks to Reggie that she had managed to narrowly escape with her life.

EPILOGUE

It was nearly dark out by the time Moira finally pulled into her driveway. She had spent hours at the police station with Reggie, getting everything straightened out and giving her statement. It was only thanks to David, who after some convincing had agreed to stay home and finish the dinner, that they had a Thanksgiving meal at all.

"I'm sorry it's so late," she said. "I made such a big deal of inviting everyone over, and I almost wrecked everything."

· · ·

"You have nothing to apologize for," Thelma said. "After what you went through today, we're just glad to see you alive."

Allison nodded. "I was so worried when my aunt called me. I can't believe someone shot at you."

"She shot at the police too, and she's going to be put away for a long time for that," Moira said grimly. "Enough of that talk, though. I just spent half the day going over what happened again and again with the police. Now I want to focus on Thanksgiving dinner with all of you."

The five of them were seated around the kitchen table. Keeva and Maverick, released from the mudroom, were pacing around the table, their noses twitching as they sniffed hopefully for a tidbit. She and David were at the head and foot of the table, with Reggie, Allison, and Thelma seated around them. The turkey was in the middle, a gorgeous, golden brown bird with stuffing inside. Around it were the casseroles, mashed potatoes, and freshly made cornbread, and sitting on the counter were the three apple pies that Thelma had brought over, along with the pumpkin pie that David had made.

"David, this looks wonderful," she said. "Thank you so much for cooking all of this."

"You don't need to thank me," he said. "This is our Thanksgiving dinner. I was happy to help. I would have done more from the beginning if you had asked."

"I know, I know," she said. "I just can't get over how wonderful everything looks. After the day I had, it's going to be amazing to dig in."

"I want to give a toast before we get started," he said. "To Moira, who solved a crime and still made it home in time for dinner."

. . .

She laughed as everyone clinked their glasses. "And I'd like to make a toast too, to David, who made the dinner possible, despite the mess I got myself into, and to Reggie, who probably saved my life with his quick thinking by calling 911 when he heard the gunshot."

There was more clinking, and everyone congratulated Reggie, who looked embarrassed.

"Thank you so much, everyone. You don't know how much it means to me for you all to be here," Moira said. "I'm so happy that I get to spend the evening with all of you."

"Thank you for inviting me," Allison said. "I think this is just what I needed. It feels good to be with everyone again. I'm sorry that I've been so withdrawn lately."

"Don't worry," Moira said. "We understand. No one blames you for being upset."

. . .

"I keep wishing that I had been able to say goodbye to my father," Allison said. "But I realized something today. I did get to say goodbye to him. Somehow, even though I never knew he existed, and he probably didn't know I did either, the universe conspired to bring us together so that he was found by someone related to him; someone who would have cared about him if she had known him. For a long time, I was so angry that I was the one that found him, but at least this way I know I was able to do something for him at least once, even if that was as simple as calling the police."

"I know it's hard," Moira said. "I'm sure it will take you a while to figure everything out. I hope you know, you have all of us. And that's why I want to make my last toast to family. Family is the people that you choose to love, not necessarily the people whose blood you share."

When the toast was done, she sipped her glass of wine then put it down. It was time to cut the turkey, give thanks, and dig into the wonderful meal. It had been a rough day, but there was nowhere else that she would rather be. Today was Thanksgiving, and she had a lot to be thankful for.

Book 15: Pretzel Pizza Murder

Book 16: Parmesan Pizza Murder

Book 17: Breakfast Pizza Murder

Book 18: Halloween Pizza Murder

Book 19: Thanksgiving Pizza Murder

Book 20: Christmas Pizza Murder

Book 21: A Crispy Slice of Murder

Book 22: Lobster Pizza Murder

Book 23: Pizza, Weddings, and Murder

Book 24: Pizza, Paradise, and Murder

Book 25: Meat Lovers and Murder

Book 26: Classic Crust Murder

Book 27: Hot, Spicy Murder

Book 28: Pork, Pizza, and Murder

Book 29: Chicken Alfredo Murder

Book 30: Jalapeño Pizza Murder

Book 31: Pesto Pizza Murder

Book 32: Sweet Chili Murder

Book 31: Shamrocks and Murder

Book 32: Sugar Coated Murder

Book 33: Murder, My Darling

Killer Cookie Series

Book 1: Killer Caramel Cookies

Book 2: Killer Halloween Cookies

Book 3: Killer Maple Cookies

Book 4: Crunchy Christmas Murder

Book 5: Killer Valentine Cookies

Asheville Meadows Series

Book 1: Small Town Murder

Book 2: Murder on Aisle Three

Book 3: The Heart of Murder

Book 4: Dating is Murder

Book 5: Dying to Cook

Book 6: Food, Family and Murder

Book 7: Fish, Chips and Murder

Cozy Mystery Tails of Alaska

Book 1: Mushing is Murder

Book 2: Murder Befalls Us

Book 3: Stage Fright and Murder

Book 4: Routine Murder

Book 5: Best Friends and Betrayal

Book 6: Tick Tock and Treachery

AUTHOR'S NOTE

I'd love to hear your thoughts on my books, the storylines, and anything else that you'd like to comment on—reader feedback is very important to me. My contact information, along with some other helpful links, is listed on the next page. If you'd like to be on my list of "folks to contact" with updates, release and sales notifications, etc.... just shoot me an email and let me know. Thanks for reading!

Also...

... if you're looking for more great reads, Summer Prescott Books publishes several popular series by outstanding Cozy Mystery authors.

CONTACT SUMMER PRESCOTT BOOKS PUBLISHING

Twitter: @summerprescott1

Bookbub: https://www.bookbub.com/authors/summer-prescott

Blog and Book Catalog: http://summerprescottbooks.com

Email: summer.prescott.cozies@gmail.com

YouTube: https://www.youtube.com/channel/UCngKNUkDdWuQ5k7-Vkfrp6A

And...be sure to check out the Summer Prescott Cozy Mysteries fan page and Summer Prescott

Books Publishing Page on Facebook – let's be friends!

To download a free book, and sign up for our fun and exciting newsletter, which will give you opportunities to win prizes and swag, enter contests, and be the first to know about New Releases, click here: http://summerprescottbooks.com

Made in United States
Troutdale, OR
12/28/2023